ENJOY MORE ADVENTURES WiTH
JASMINE TOGUCHI

Jasmine Toguchi, Mochi Queen

JASMINE TOGUCHI
SUPER SLEUTH

MINE
GUCHI

SUPER
SLEUTH

DEBBI MICHIKO FLORENCE   PICTURES BY ELIZABET VUKOVIĆ

FARRAR STRAUS GIROUX • NEW YORK

Farrar Straus Giroux Books for Young Readers
An imprint of Macmillan Publishing Group, LLC
175 Fifth Avenue, New York, NY 10010

Printed in the United States of America by
LSC Communications, Harrisonburg, Virginia
Designed by Kristie Radwilowicz
First edition, 2017
Hardcover: 10 9 8 7 6 5 4 3 2 1
Paperback: 10 9 8 7 6 5 4 3 2 1

mackids.com

Library of Congress Cataloging-in-Publication Data

Names: Florence, Debbi Michiko, author. | Vuković, Elizabet, illustrator.
Title: Jasmine Toguchi, super sleuth / Debbi Michiko Florence ; illustrations
    by Elizabet Vuković.
Description: First edition. | New York : Farrar Straus Giroux, 2017. |
    Series: Jasmine Toguchi | Summary: Jasmine has looked forward to spending
    Girl's Day with her family and best friend, Linnie, but first her sister
    says she will not participate, and then Jasmine upsets Linnie. |
    Description based on print version record and CIP data provided by
    publisher; resource not viewed.
Identifiers: LCCN 2016038113 (print) | LCCN 2017017614 (ebook) | ISBN
    9780374304157 (Ebook) | ISBN 9780374304133 (hardcover) | ISBN
    9780974308353 (pbk.)
Subjects: | CYAC: Family life—Fiction. | Best friends—Fiction. |
    Friendship—Fiction. | Holidays—Fiction. | Japanese Americans—Fiction.
Classification: LCC PZ7.1.F593 (ebook) | LCC PZ7.1.F593 Jas 2017 (print) |
    DDC [E]—dc23
LC record available at https://lccn.loc.gov/2016038113

Our books may be purchased for promotional, educational, or
business use. Please contact your local bookseller or the Macmillan
Corporate and Premium Sales Department at (800) 221-7945
ext. 5442 or by e-mail at MacmillanSpecialMarkets@macmillan.com.

FOR MY SISTER, GAIL HIROKANE,
WITH LOVE —D.M.F.

FOR KATA, MY MOM, WHOSE FABRIC
CREATIONS SHOWED ME THAT WHAT
YOU START OUT WITH ISN'T ALL THAT
YOU CAN END UP WITH —E.V.

CONTENTS

Big
PLANS

Bing bong bong bing!

Ms. Sanchez played the end-of-the-day song on her xylophone. It was time to clean up and get ready to go home. Normally I do *not* like to clean, but today was different. I was looking forward to the end of school.

Because I, Jasmine Toguchi, had *big* weekend plans!

I was excited for my best friend, Linnie Green, to come over to my house. Usually on

Fridays, she walked home with her babysitter, Marcy. But Marcy, who is in high school, was sick. Hooray! Not that I wanted Marcy to be sick. That would be mean, and one of Mom's rules is to be nice. But this way Linnie could come to my house.

My classmates took out their notebooks. Normally after Ms. Sanchez played her end-of-the-day song, she gave us our homework assignment. I was the only person who did not take out her notebook, because I knew better.

Maggie Milsap raised her hand. "Ms. Sanchez! Jasmine doesn't have her notebook."

Everyone turned to look at me.

"Did you forget it, Jasmine?" Ms. Sanchez asked.

"No, Ms. Sanchez," I said. "It's in my desk."

Ms. Sanchez smiled. "Is there a reason you're not taking it out?"

"Yes," I said, "because you're not giving us homework."

"You aren't a mind reader," Maggie Milsap said.

"No," I said. "But when Ms. Sanchez is going to give us homework, she puts her blue notebook on the desk. When she isn't going to give us homework, she doesn't take out the blue notebook."

Ms. Sanchez nodded. "Jasmine has outstanding observation skills. She would make an excellent detective. Class, what does *detective* mean?"

Ms. Sanchez was sneaky, always finding ways to teach us stuff. *Detective* was one of our vocabulary words.

Hands shot in the air, including mine. Ms. Sanchez called on me and I answered. "A detective is someone who solves mysteries by using clues. Another word for detective is *sleuth*."

I tossed in the last part because I learned that from my mom. Mom is an editor, a person who helps writers with their words. Mom loves words like Ms. Sanchez loves

books or music, and she's always sharing new words with me and my big sister, Sophie.

"Very good!" Ms. Sanchez said. "And Jasmine is right. Today there is no homework!"

Everyone cheered. I cheered extra-loud because this weekend was important. No homework meant free time for my big plans! Not only was Linnie sleeping over on Saturday, but we were celebrating Girl's Day together for the first time on Sunday!

MY BEST FRIEND, LiNNiE GREEN

I pulled my purple backpack onto my shoulders and followed my classmates from room 5 out to the tree by the parking lot. That's where we waited every day to be picked up by our parents or guardians.

Even though the sun was shining, it was cold outside for March. Mrs. Reese, my neighbor, called winter in Los Angeles warm. She moved here from Vermont, where it snows a lot. I shivered just thinking about that.

Linnie came over to stand with me.

"What are you two doing this afternoon?" Ms. Sanchez asked us.

"Not homework," I said.

Ms. Sanchez laughed. "Yes, you are good at paying attention to clues. That's a great skill to have, Jasmine."

That made me feel warm and fizzy inside. "Maybe I will be a detective when I grow up," I said. I really wanted to have a flamingo farm, because flamingos are my favorite bird. But maybe I could do both.

"I'm spending the afternoon at Jasmine's house," Linnie said. "She's going to show me her special Girl's Day dolls."

"And Linnie is coming back to my house on Saturday for a sleepover," I said, grinning.

"That sounds like fun," Ms. Sanchez said.

"I'm so excited!" Linnie slipped her hand into mine and squeezed. "Sunday, March 3, is Girl's Day, a Japanese celebration for girls."

Linnie is not Japanese-American like I am, but because she is my very best friend, she knows stuff about me. Just like I know she celebrates Hanukkah instead of Christmas.

We weren't always best friends. When I started first grade, I didn't even know who Linnie Green was.

In class, we had to choose one thing to do a report on. I chose rocks. Another girl picked rocks, too. It was Linnie. And the teacher made us partners.

Every day at recess and every day after school, Linnie and I searched for rocks. We looked on the playground and we looked at the park. We looked in my backyard and we looked in *her* backyard. After five days, we had a big collection. We had smooth rocks and rough rocks, big stones and little pebbles, gray rocks and black rocks. One was pink and oval, like an egg.

When we showed our rocks to the class, the teacher gave us two smiley-face stickers for doing a great job. Even better, Linnie and I became best friends.

Linnie collects rocks, so I let her keep them. Whenever I see a pretty one, I give it to Linnie.

The pink oval rock is her favorite of all. Sometimes she lets me hold it and pretend it is a flamingo egg.

"How wonderful that there's a special day for girls," Ms. Sanchez said.

"There's a different celebration for boys, too," I said. "But we don't have any boys in our family, except for my dad."

"Do you do anything special for Girl's Day?" Ms. Sanchez asked.

"Yes," I said. "We put out dolls of the Japanese imperial court, like the emperor and empress."

"And Jasmine gets to dress up in a kimono," Linnie said. "A kimono is a special Japanese outfit like a robe, but fancier and prettier."

"Well, I hope you girls have a wonderful celebration," Ms. Sanchez said.

"We will," I said. This was going to be the most wonderful weekend!

MRS. REESE'S 8ARA8E

When we got home, I took Linnie to the living room to see the imperial court.

She knelt in front of the doll display. "This is so cool," she said. "I love their fancy out-fits."

Every year, Dad put the wooden steps together and covered them with red felt. Then Sophie and I helped Mom arrange the dolls. Except Mom was the only one allowed to touch the dolls because they were made out of ceramic. Also, they belong to Mom. But before they were hers, they belonged to Obaachan, my grandma. One day, those dolls would be Sophie's because she is the older daughter. But Mom promised she would buy me my very own set when I grew up.

I loved to watch Mom place hats on the heads of the dolls and fans in their hands. She slid swords under their arms. Then she carefully positioned each doll in its proper place. The dolls wore fancy kimonos made from silk.

Sophie and I arranged the less delicate things, like the trees and the trays with miniature bowls and cups. For some reason, Mom did not trust Sophie and me with the dolls. Maybe it was because when Sophie was seven and I was five, we once moved all the dolls to the floor so they could sit around the trees and have a picnic. Mom was not happy. At least we didn't break anything.

"That's the emperor and the empress on the top level," I explained to Linnie. "And those are the ladies of the court, the musicians, the ministers, and the guards." I pointed to each row.

"Their outfits are pretty," Linnie said. "I wish I could wear a kimono on Sunday, too."

One of Linnie's favorite things to do is play dress up. At her house, we put on her old Halloween costumes and pretend we live in a magical kingdom.

I smiled a secret smile. I didn't tell Linnie that Mom had a kimono for her to wear on Girl's Day. It was Sophie's old kimono she'd outgrown. I couldn't wait to surprise Linnie!

Until this year, we had only celebrated as a family. But Linnie is my very best friend, and I wanted to share this day with her. I was happy Mom let me invite her.

I sucked in a breath. I had another surprise for Linnie. "We can dress up in other clothes right now, if you want," I said.

"Really?" she asked.

"Really! My neighbor Mrs. Reese has boxes and boxes of clothes. She told me I could play with them anytime I want," I said.

Linnie clapped her hands. "Let's go!"

We raced from the living room to the

kitchen. I just had to check in with Mom. "We're going to Mrs. Reese's to play in her garage," I said quickly.

"The clothes are in her garage?" Linnie asked.

Mom lifted a finger while she finished writing on a page. She worked part of her time at an office and part of her time at home. When she was done, she looked at her watch. "I'll call you back in an hour."

When I played at Mrs. Reese's, all Mom had to do was step outside and yell my name. The rule was that I had to come home right when she called for me. Sometimes I pretended not to hear her until she used my full name. When she called out *Jasmine Toguchi*, I knew she meant serious business.

"We don't have to go," Linnie said. "We can play in your room."

"Don't worry," I said. "An hour is plenty of time to play dress up!"

I took Linnie's hand and we walked two houses over to Mrs. Reese's.

Usually I climbed over the gate because it was fun, but Linnie didn't like to climb. She was afraid of falling. So I opened the gate to the backyard instead.

I glanced at the apricot tree. This was my special thinking tree. Mrs. Reese lets me climb it whenever I need a place to think. It would be fun to share it with Linnie, but like I said, Linnie does *not* like to climb.

Mrs. Reese's garage was special, too. I had the smallest room at our house, not that I minded a whole lot, but this garage was like a private room all my own. Mrs. Reese never opened the big door for cars. Around the side of the garage was a regular door.

"It's dark in there," Linnie said, twirling her finger around a strand of her brown hair.

The windows were dusty, but some light shone in. Towers of plastic boxes looked like trees in a forest. In the center of the garage, a giant dresser with four big drawers sat like a castle. I loved it in here!

DRESSING UP

I went into the garage and turned on the light. Linnie poked her head in. Ever since Mrs. Reese told me last month that I could play in here, I came every Saturday. I hadn't had a chance to open all the boxes yet, but I knew what was in the dresser. I tugged open the bottom drawer and pulled out a silver dress.

"Look, Linnie," I said, holding it up. "You can be a princess!" At her house, she was usually the princess and I was usually the knight.

She was in front of me in a flash. I helped

Linnie put it on, and the short dress became a gown on her.

"Wowee zowee! You look fabulous!" I squealed.

"Ms. Sanchez said you'd make a good detective. Why don't you find the perfect private-eye outfit?" Linnie said.

"Good idea!" I agreed.

Linnie searched through the dresser for princess shoes while I walked to the back of the garage. I opened a box and shook out a cape. It wasn't a superhero cape in bright red, but a black cape, like a magician's. I tied it around my neck. Maybe I could find a wand and be a magical detective.

I dug in the box. Black boots. Green-and-red scarf. An explorer helmet with a light in front! I put that on even though it didn't match my cape. A detective needs a good flashlight anyhow.

At the very bottom of the box was a scarf made of pink feathers, like a flamingo!

Flamingos are bright pink birds with long legs. Just looking at them makes me happy. Having my very own pet flamingo would make me happier. But Mom says flamingos belong in the wild and wouldn't make good pets. I think a flamingo would be perfectly happy living with me!

I wrapped the scarf around my neck. "Linnie," I called out. "I'm a magic exploring flamingo detective!" All good things.

Linnie peered around some boxes. "It's dark back here."

I waved her over. "There's plenty of light," I said. I tried to switch on the bulb on my hat but it didn't work. Too bad.

"Maybe we should go back to your house," she said in a quiet voice.

"But we're not done," I said. "There are more clothes we can try on!" I opened another box.

"Why does your neighbor have so many outfits?" Linnie asked.

"I don't know," I said. I never thought about asking her. "Maybe it's a secret!"

Linnie said, "Maybe she has a secret past!"

"Maybe she was a *spy*," I whispered. "And these were her disguises! Maybe she had to leave Vermont because her enemies were about to find out who she was!"

"That's so cool," Linnie said.

I tried to picture Mrs. Reese in the explorer's helmet I was wearing. Nope. Then I tried to picture her in the silvery dress. That was hard to imagine, too. And I have a very good imagination.

"I wish we could find out for sure," Linnie said.

I waved my cape. "I am a super sleuth. I will solve the mystery of Mrs. Reese's past!"

Suddenly, the garage turned darker.

Linnie moved closer to me. "I think it's time for us to go back to your house."

I shook my head. "It's not late. The sun just went behind some clouds. Let's look for clues!"

"If we hurry, can we go home soon?" Linnie asked.

"Definitely," I said as I opened a third box.

We searched through boxes and drawers, pulling out all sorts of things. I wasn't sure what kind of clue I was looking for, but I'd know it when I saw it.

"Jasmine!" Mom's voice came from outside. "It's time to come home!"

"Oh, Jasmine," Linnie said. "What a mess."

I looked around. Clothes and hats and purses and jewelry were scattered all over the place.

Usually I do not mind a mess so much, but this was a real disaster.

"Oh, no," I said. "Mrs. Reese has a rule that I have to put everything away neatly."

"Jasmine!" Mom's voice got louder.

"I don't think we have time to put everything away," Linnie said.

"Jasmine! Come home!" Mom's voice was even louder now.

I knew one thing for sure: I did *not* want Mom to see this mess. She did not like messes.

"Let's go," Linnie said.

"I can't leave everything out," I said, hopping around, trying to shake out my nervousness.

"But your mom is calling," Linnie said.

"Quick," I said. "Just shove everything wherever it will go, out of sight."

I grabbed a bunch of clothes off the dresser and crammed them into a drawer. I pushed and pushed until the drawer shut. A piece of green dress poked out, but I did not have time to worry about that.

"Jasmine Toguchi!" Mom's voice was closer.

"Hurry, Linnie!" I shouted as I threw another handful of clothes into a box and slammed the lid down.

Linnie scooped up shoes and hats. I

snatched off my costume, then helped Linnie take off hers. We stuffed them into the last box.

"Jasmine?" Mom opened the door.

"We're cleaning up, Mom," I said.

Mom squinted and looked around. I looked around, too. My heart rammed my ribs so hard it hurt my chest. Everything looked fine. No clothes or hats on the floor. The boxes were closed and stacked. I kicked a shoe under the dresser.

"Good job, girls," Mom said. "Now let's go. Linnie's mother will be here soon."

Linnie ran after my mom while I turned off the light. Everything looked okay, but I knew that inside the dresser and those boxes the clothes were a messy jumble. I thought about my promise to Mrs. Reese. My insides felt jumbled, too.

TOO OLD
FOR DOLLS

On Saturday, I woke up to a delicious smell.
I hopped out of bed and ran to the kitchen.
Every weekend, we have family-time break-
fast. Dad makes banana pancakes.

"Ohayo-gozai-masu!" I said good morning
to Dad in Japanese. I didn't speak Japanese
like my mom and dad, but I knew some words.

"Good morning, Jasmine," Dad said as he
flipped a golden pancake.

Mom was pouring orange juice. Sophie,

who was not a morning person, was slumped over in her chair. I used my observation skills and saw that her elbows were on the table. I nudged her as I sat down. Mom did not like elbows on the table. Sophie glared at me, but she sat up.

Dad taught history at a college. He said people could learn from history. History didn't always mean stuff from a long time ago, like before cars. History could be newer, too. Like how Sophie spilled orange juice last week when she bumped it with her elbow. Mom doesn't forget any kind of history easily. Sophie wasn't as good about remembering.

That reminded me of what I learned from my own history. One time, I promised Mom I would clean up after I made a collage in the kitchen. I make collages by cutting out pictures and words from magazines and gluing them onto cardboard. That time, I didn't clean up. I'm not allowed to make collages at the kitchen table anymore. What if Mrs. Reese found out I didn't clean up the clothes in the garage? Would she tell me I couldn't play in there anymore?

Suddenly, I wished it were a school-morning kind of breakfast. Those breakfasts were quick. I needed to get to Mrs. Reese's garage before she had a chance to check on it.

As soon as Mom and Dad sat down, I took my fork and speared a pancake off the serving platter. I smeared butter on top. I skipped the syrup.

"Ita-daki-masu," I said. It was what we said in Japanese before we ate. It meant thank you for the meal.

I shoved a big bite of pancake into my mouth and asked, "Can I go to Mrs. Reese's this morning?" But it sounded like "Dan I go to Mrtth. Reeth's dis morning?"

"Ew," Sophie said. "Say it, don't spray it."

"Jasmine," Dad said. "Please swallow your food before you talk."

I chewed superfast.

"Jasmine," Mom said. "What is wrong with you?"

I chewed some more and swallowed. I took a big gulp of my orange juice. I coughed from drinking it too fast. Mom patted my back.

"Jasmine Toguchi," Mom said. "Please slow down."

"I want to get to Mrs. Reese's garage."

"Linnie is coming over for the sleepover," Mom said. "Why don't you wait until she arrives?"

I really didn't want to wait, even though I was excited about Linnie coming. But maybe with Linnie's help I could clean up the garage faster! That made me feel better.

"Sophie," Mom said, "are your friends coming, too?"

Sophie shrugged. "I'm too old to do Girl's Day."

"What?" I said, forgetting to finish chewing. "What do you mean?"

Sophie and I always celebrated Girl's Day with Mom. It was a tradition. Tradition means something you do regularly. Like when we get to open one present on Christmas Eve and all the rest on Christmas morning. Or when we make mochi, a Japanese sweet treat, with the entire family every New Year's.

On Girl's Day, Sophie and I dress up in kimonos and Mom takes pictures of us by the doll display. After a special snack, Mom, Sophie, and I usually do something fun together,

just us girls. Last year, we went to the zoo and I got to see flamingos!

Sophie and I try to convince Mom to give us presents, too, but Mom always says, *That's not what Girl's Day is about.* Too bad.

"It's our tradition," I said to Sophie.

"I'm too old for dolls," Sophie replied. She flipped her hair over her shoulder, something she had just started doing a lot.

"You know it's not only about dolls, Sophie," Mom said. "It's about celebrating girls. I love celebrating with my daughters."

Sophie shook her head. "I really don't want to, Mom."

Mom's eyes looked sad, but Sophie didn't seem to notice. I felt sad, too. Ever since Sophie started fifth grade, she had stopped playing with me. I thought at least on Girl's Day she would be around.

WHAT A MESS

I didn't have time to worry about that now, though, because I was too busy worrying about Mrs. Reese discovering the mess in her garage. Fortunately, Linnie came over soon after breakfast. The minute she walked in the door, I grabbed her arm and dragged her down the hall into my room.

"Whoa, I guess we're both excited!" Linnie said.

She put her overnight bag on my bed and

held on to a smaller purple bag with handles. Normally I would ask her what was in there. Normally I would be very curious. But right now was not a normally time.

"We have to go back to Mrs. Reese's garage right now," I said.

Linnie froze like we were playing statue tag. "Why?" she asked.

"We need to put everything back neatly. Then we can play more dress up and solve the mystery of Mrs. Reese's boxes of clothes!" I hopped around the room, twice on my left foot, twice on my right, and then back to my left foot again. Dad said moving was a good way to get rid of nerves and energy.

Linnie frowned. "I thought we could do something else today. I brought my paper dolls," she said. "We can make clothes for them."

"We can do that after we clean up the garage. We both made the mess, so it's fair that we both clean it up."

Linnie looked down at my floor. "Okay. You're right."

"Yes!" I pumped my fist. "Let's hurry!"

After I told Mom we were going to Mrs. Reese's, I ran two houses over. Linnie walked. I dashed up Mrs. Reese's driveway. Linnie was

walking superslow and was far behind me. I scrambled over the gate.

The side door to the garage was open and the light was on. My feet seemed as heavy as stones suddenly. I crept up to the door, nibbling my lip as I peeked inside.

In the garage, Mrs. Reese shook out a wrinkled dress and smoothed it. Then she folded the dress just like she taught me when she first showed me all the boxes. She picked up a crunched straw hat. My heart felt crunched, too.

Walnuts! I was too late. Mrs. Reese would be angry with me. She would tell me I couldn't play in here anymore. Maybe she would tell me I couldn't have my secret thinking spot in her tree anymore either. My throat was tight, like it had something stuck in it. My eyes and nose tickled with tears.

"It wasn't me!" I blurted out.

Mrs. Reese turned around. "Well, hello, Jasmine."

She didn't look angry, but my eyes were blurry and I couldn't see very well.

"I wanted to clean up yesterday, but my friend Linnie didn't want to," I said. "It's her fault everything is a mess!"

"Jasmine!"

I turned around. Linnie stood behind me, her face full of surprise and hurt. My heart fluttered like a trapped butterfly. I had never seen Linnie's face look like that before. Like I had slapped her.

"Girls," Mrs. Reese said, "it's okay. I'm just looking for a special hat for my daughter. Did you see a black hat with a peacock feather?"

I shook my head. "No, but we can help you find it." If I helped Mrs. Reese, maybe she would forget I had broken her rule.

"That would be great," Mrs. Reese said. "Do you have time right now to look with me?"

"No!" Linnie shouted, and ran away.

A LOT OF PROBLEMS

I told Mrs. Reese I would be right back, then I ran home.

I found Linnie in the living room. She was sitting on the couch, holding my favorite book, *Charlotte's Web*. My bookmark was on the table. I could tell by the way she was holding the book open smack against her face that she wasn't really reading. I didn't need to be a detective to know Linnie was upset.

I shuffled my feet on the rug and tried to think of something to say. "Do you want to go

back to Mrs. Reese's? She doesn't seem mad at us."

Linnie turned a page. I hoped she wouldn't lose my place.

"Do you want to make a collage?" I asked.

Linnie turned another page, even though she couldn't possibly read that fast.

"Well, how about we make costumes for your paper dolls?" I knew Linnie wanted to do that.

Linnie kept pretending to read.

I sat down next to her. "You said you wanted to make doll costumes."

She didn't answer. My face got hot and my insides churned. "Linnie, talk to me!"

Finally, she put the book down. "You lied, Jasmine!" Linnie scrunched her hands into fists. "You told Mrs. Reese it was *my* fault that we didn't clean up."

"It wasn't a lie," I said. "You wanted to leave when my mom called for us!"

"It was *your* idea to throw everything in boxes," she said, her voice squeaking.

"It doesn't matter," I said. "Mrs. Reese isn't mad. We can go back and help her find that hat. And maybe we can find clues about her mysterious past." I wiggled my eyebrows, hoping to make Linnie laugh. She didn't.

"I don't care about that," Linnie said, crossing her arms.

"Well, I don't care about your paper dolls!" I crossed my arms, too. My skin prickled.

Mom walked into the room. "Would you girls like a snack?" Obviously Mom didn't have very good observation skills.

"Yes, please, Mrs. Toguchi," Linnie said, uncrossing her arms.

In the kitchen, Mom gave us plates of cookies and sat down with us. "We're so happy you're here for Girl's Day, Linnie."

"Actually, I need to go home," Linnie said, not looking up.

The air whooshed out of me.

"Now?" Mom sounded surprised. "Aren't you sleeping over so we can celebrate Girl's Day tomorrow?"

Linnie looked at me. I looked at my uneaten chocolate chip cookie. Mom made a small sound, like she was trying to figure things out.

"Did Jasmine upset you?" Mom asked.

After a long moment, Linnie said, "Yes. She hurt my feelings." Linnie picked at her cookie.

"She told Mrs. Reese it was my fault that the clothes weren't put away right."

Linnie was snitching on me! She was not a good friend at all.

"Jasmine Toguchi, go to your room," Mom said. "Linnie, if you really want to go home, I will take you."

"I really do," she said in a small voice.

★　★　★

Linnie did not say goodbye. I did not say goodbye. I went straight to my room.

I paced and paced. One bad thing about having the smallest room in the house (except for the bathroom) was that it was hard to pace. I circled around and around. Pacing helped me think when I couldn't climb my thinking tree. Just like hopping helped me get my energy out.

Linnie was mad at me, but I was mad at

her, too! Who needed her? Not me! I could do things without her, like figure out if Mrs. Reese was a spy. Ms. Sanchez said I had good observation skills. *I* was the great detective. I would solve the mystery all by myself!

I peeked out the window. Mom's car wasn't back yet. I could go to Mrs. Reese's right now before Mom got back. I opened my door. Sophie sat in the hall.

"Where do you think you're going?" Sophie asked.

"Mrs. Reese's garage," I said.

"I don't know why you like playing in there. That garage is super-creepy," Sophie said.

I shrugged. Sophie slept with a night-light because she was afraid of the dark. It didn't surprise me she didn't want to play in Mrs.

Reese's garage. Not that she would play with me anyway.

"Mom told me to make sure you stayed in the house until she got back," Sophie said.

I sucked on my lip. Before Sophie started fifth grade, she would have been on my side and I could have snuck away. But not anymore. I missed the old Sophie. "Why won't you celebrate Girl's Day tomorrow?" I asked.

"Already told you. It's for kids," she said.

"No. Mom said *all* girls celebrate it in Japan. Daughters with their mothers and grandmothers," I said.

A car door slammed. Mom was home! I slipped back into my room and shut the door. When Dad closed the door to his office, it meant not to disturb him. Maybe if I kept my door closed, Mom wouldn't disturb me.

No such luck.

Mom knocked on my door and opened it. "I spoke to Mrs. Reese," Mom said, stepping into my room. "Fortunately for you, she isn't upset about the mess you left. Unfortunately, you hurt Linnie's feelings and she *is* really upset."

"Is she coming back?" I asked, sitting on my bed.

"I'm afraid not." Mom saw Linnie's overnight bag on my bed. "Oh, dear. Linnie forgot her stuff."

I didn't say anything.

Mom leaned against my door. "I'm not sure we should celebrate Girl's Day at this point. Between Sophie not wanting to participate and you not being a good friend, I'm disappointed."

I slid off the bed and onto the floor, like a leaf falling from a tree. I wished I could drift away.

"Go back to Mrs. Reese's and clean up your mess," Mom said. "Do not play dress up. Come straight home when you're done. Got it?"

"Got it," I whispered.

I had a lot of problems. Mom was angry with me for upsetting Linnie. I was mad at Linnie for saying it wasn't her fault when it was at least *partly* her fault. I wanted to help Mrs. Reese find that hat to make up for leaving a mess. Linnie wasn't coming back over. Sophie didn't want to celebrate Girl's Day. And now Mom might not want to either. Everything was getting ruined!

SLEUTHING FOR CLUES

The garage was dark and empty when I got there. I turned on the light and looked in the drawers and boxes. All the clothes were folded and put away neatly. My stomach twisted like I'd eaten some disgusting nuts.

I went to the back door and knocked. When Mrs. Reese answered, she smiled at me.

"Welcome back, Jasmine," she said, letting me into the kitchen.

"I'm sorry for not cleaning up," I said. It was very hard to say sorry. It was the same as saying, *I messed up.* I did not like to mess up.

Mrs. Reese smiled. "It's okay, Jasmine. I understand that sometimes you run out of time."

At least Mrs. Reese wasn't angry. I took a big breath. "I was supposed to help you put everything away," I said.

"I finished," Mrs. Reese said, sitting down at her kitchen table. "But you can help me find that peacock hat."

"I'll look for it right now!" I said. Finally, something I could do to help.

"Where is your friend?" Mrs. Reese asked.

"She went home." I frowned. "We're not friends anymore."

"I'm sorry to hear that," Mrs. Reese said. "Good friends are important. I hope you two will make up very soon."

I didn't know how that would happen, since Linnie wasn't sleeping over anymore. But maybe if I solved the mystery, I would have something to share with Linnie. Maybe then she wouldn't stay mad at me.

I knew from movies and books that a real spy wouldn't tell the truth about what she did. So asking Mrs. Reese wasn't going to work. I was going to have to become a super sleuth.

"I will find that hat for you all by myself," I said.

"Thank you." Mrs. Reese smiled.

Back in the garage, I put my hands on my hips. The hat wouldn't be in the boxes Linnie and I had opened. I have a good memory, and I hadn't seen a black hat with a peacock feather yesterday. I went over to the boxes I hadn't opened yet.

The first one was full of clothes, but no hats. I closed that box and moved on to the next one. Instead of clothes, there were stacks of folders. I almost closed that box, too, when I remembered I was also looking for clues. These might be evidence!

In one of the folders was a stack of papers with neat handwriting. I read out loud, *"Three pairs of white gloves. Leather coat. Black bow tie. Sixteen aprons."* On every

sheet of paper was a list of clothes. Could these be Mrs. Reese's shopping lists for her disguises? Why would she need so many aprons?

Under that folder was a stack of colorful flyers. They looked like movie posters, but not for any movies I'd ever heard of. *Annie Get Your Gun.* That sounded dangerous! *Fiddler on the Roof.* That sounded like fun. I would love to climb up on a

roof, but Mom would prob-
ably get mad if I did. *Oklahoma!* That was a state,
like California.

What did these mean?
Were they messages? Or
scrap paper? Or maybe
titles of books? I wished Linnie were here to
help me figure it out. I put the papers back in
the box.

I reached into a third box. Something tickled my hand. I pulled out a hat with a feather.
Wowee zowee! I'd found it! I grinned and did
a little hopping dance.

I ran back into Mrs. Reese's house.

"Is this what you're looking for?" I asked.

Mrs. Reese smiled. "It
is! Thank you, Jasmine!
My daughter will be very
happy."

I was glad Mrs. Reese

and I were still friends. Now if only I could be friends with Linnie again.

"I hear you're having a celebration tomorrow," Mrs. Reese said, taking the peacock hat from me.

"Yes," I said. "Well, maybe."

"Maybe?" she asked.

"Tomorrow *is* Girl's Day, but right now Sophie doesn't want to celebrate, and Linnie is upset with me, and Mom is disappointed. So we might not celebrate at all," I said.

"I'm sorry to hear that," Mrs. Reese said. "It sounds like such a wonderful holiday, to celebrate girls. I wish I had something like that with my daughter when she was growing up."

I nodded.

"I hope you get to celebrate after all, Jasmine," Mrs. Reese said.

I hoped so, too, but I didn't have a good feeling about it. I needed to talk with Linnie or it would not be a good Girl's Day. Not at all.

A DISCOVERY

When I got home, I grabbed the phone and went to my room. I decided to call Linnie before I chickened out. Her phone rang. One time. Two times. Three times. Maybe she wasn't home.

On the fourth ring, someone picked up.

"Hello?" Linnie's voice was so quiet I had to press the phone hard against my ear to hear her.

"Hi," I said. "It's me. Jasmine."

Silence. Maybe she hadn't heard me. I spoke louder. "Hi, Linnie!"

Nothing. I gripped the phone. "Guess what?" I said. "I found some clues in Mrs. Reese's garage! I think she really was a spy!"

Linnie still didn't say anything, but I could hear her breathing. "Don't you want to know about the clues I found?"

"I am not talking to you, Jasmine Toguchi," she finally said. "I am really mad at you!"

And then she hung up!

I didn't know what to do. I paced my room in tiny circles until I got too dizzy. I sat down on my bed. How could Linnie hang up on me? Best friends don't hang up on each other.

They do fun things together. Like Sophie and her best friend, Maya Fung. They talk on the phone. They paint their nails the same color. They bake cookies together. They like to do all the same things, *together*.

But Linnie and I didn't like all the same

things. Her favorite color was green and mine was purple. Linnie liked to do puzzles. I liked to make collages. Linnie played the piano. I didn't play anything. We were not alike. All of a sudden, I didn't know why we were friends at all.

I stood up and started pacing again, but immediately tripped on something. Tangled around my foot was the pretty purple bag Linnie had brought over. I had forgotten to ask about it. It looked like a gift bag. I untangled the handles from my foot. The bag was so heavy that it *clunk*ed when I put it on my desk. I reached in and pulled out Linnie's pink oval rock. It fit perfectly in my hand.

I peeked into the bag. There was an envelope with my name on it. I opened it and read the note.

Dear Jasmine,
    Happy Girl's Day! You are my very bestest friend in the world. I want you to have my special rock. I hope it really is a flamingo egg so you can finally have your pet flamingo. You are fun and nice and, most of all, brave. You help me be brave when I am afraid.

                    Your friend,
                    Linnie Green

I squeezed the rock. I read the note again. Linnie called me *brave*. I guess because I liked to climb and she didn't. Linnie was afraid of falling. Kind of like Sophie. Sophie didn't

like to climb either. She was afraid sometimes, too. Sophie didn't like the dark and she didn't like Mrs. Reese's garage.

Wait a minute. I thought hard.

On Friday, when Linnie found out we were going to Mrs. Reese's garage, she wanted to play in my room. When we got to the garage, Linnie didn't go in until I turned on the light. She complained it was too dark. When Mom called for us, Linnie wished to leave so badly that she didn't want to stay and clean up, and Linnie usually *likes* cleaning up.

Linnie was afraid of the garage!

I had missed some important clues.

I read Linnie's note again. I sucked on my bottom lip. She called me her *very bestest friend.* She gave me her favorite rock as a Girl's Day present, even though it wasn't a present-giving holiday. That's the kind of good friend she was.

Linnie and I both liked to dress up and play with dolls. We both liked rocks. I liked listening to her play the piano, and she always listened to me talk about my future pet flamingo. I missed her.

Sometimes friends don't have to like all the same things. Sometimes friends don't need to be exactly alike. It was better to have fun together. Linnie called me *brave*, but I was afraid. I was afraid Linnie would be mad at me forever. I was afraid she would not be my friend anymore. I needed to make things right.

THE BRAVE ONE

I picked up the phone and called Linnie again. When she answered I talked superfast so she couldn't hang up on me.

"Linnie, it's me, Jasmine, and I know you're really mad at me but you probably need your things since you're not sleeping over anymore and my mom is making your favorite dinner and it would hurt her feelings if you didn't come and eat with us so please come for dinner and you don't have to talk to me or anything if you don't want to but I really hope you come over." Whew. That was a lot to say in one breath.

I waited and waited. Finally, I heard Linnie say softly, "Okay." Then she hung up.

★ ★ ★

"What do you mean we have to make yakisoba for dinner?" Mom asked.

"Please, Mom, it's very important!" I leaned on the kitchen counter where Mom was unpacking groceries.

"What's going on?" she asked.

"I invited Linnie back over, and I kind of told her you were making her favorite dinner," I said.

"You're trying to make up

with Linnie. That's good." Mom stacked cans in the pantry.

"I'm going to try to convince her to stay over and celebrate Girl's Day with us," I said.

"Well, in that case, I'll make yakisoba," Mom said. "I hope Linnie agrees to stay."

I walked around the counter to hug Mom with my strong mochi-making arms. "Thank you sooo much."

Mom hugged me back. "You're welcome, sweetheart."

Now I just hoped my plan would work.

* * *

When Linnie arrived, she didn't say a word. She followed me to my room. I stood by my desk and took a deep breath. I held the flamingo rock behind my back and I squeezed it to make me braver. Linnie sat on my bed. That was a good sign. At least she didn't just grab her bag and leave.

"I'm sorry I hurt your feelings," I said. "I shouldn't have said it was your fault the garage was a mess."

I took the rock from behind my back. "I saw the present you left for me. I love this rock, but I know it's your favorite, too. You don't have to give it to me if you don't want to anymore. I am not a good friend after all."

"I want you to have it," she said.

I sat down next to Linnie. "You called me *brave*, but I think you're the brave one."

"I am?" Linnie looked surprised.

"Yes. You were brave enough to come play with me in the garage even though you didn't want to," I said.

Linnie tugged on her hair. "I was a little scared of playing in there. It was dark."

"Ms. Sanchez said I had good observation skills, but I didn't figure out how you felt until today," I said.

"You were so excited about playing in there," Linnie said. "I wanted you to be happy."

"I miss you," I said softly. "I want to be friends again. I'm *really* sorry for blaming you for the mess."

Linnie stopped tugging on her hair. "I miss you, too. I don't want to fight," she finally said.

I smiled. "Does that mean you'll stay for Girl's Day?"

"Yes!"

"Awesome!" I leaped off the bed and started hopping. "I'm so happy we're best friends!"

We grinned at each other. Then we fell into a giggling fit.

FIGURING IT OUT

"I think we were right about Mrs. Reese being a spy," I said when I finally caught my breath.

"Really?"

"I found papers in a box," I said. "They looked like little posters and said *Annie Get Your Gun, Fiddler on the Roof*, and *Oklahoma!*"

"What does that mean?" Linnie asked.

"I don't know," I said. "I think they might be messages. Like a code."

"Is her name Annie?" Linnie asked.

"Maybe. So maybe the message was for her to get her gun and dress up as a fiddler and meet the person on a roof in Oklahoma!"

"That's amazing!" Linnie said. "You are so smart, Jasmine."

"What are you guys doing?" Sophie asked from my doorway.

"We figured out that Mrs. Reese used to be a spy," I said.

Sophie flipped her hair. "Yeah, right."

"It's true," Linnie said. "Those clothes in her garage are her disguises. Jasmine found coded messages for disguises like a fiddler on a roof."

Sophie grinned. "Like that musical!"

"What do you mean?" I asked.

Sophie walked into my room and sat down

at my desk. This was the first time she had come into my room in, like, forever!

"Did you see if Mom bought the special mochi for Girl's Day?" she asked.

"No," I said. "But I know she went to the store today. Why?"

"No reason. I just hope she didn't buy one for me, since I'm not celebrating." Sophie stood back up and walked over to my door. "But," she said, turning back to me, "if she *did* buy an extra, make sure you save it for me."

Then Sophie left as quickly as she had come. "That was weird," I said.

"Very," Linnie agreed. "Do you want to make costumes for my paper dolls?"

"Yes!" I was relieved Linnie and I were friends again.

We took her paper dolls out of her overnight bag, and I dug in my desk drawer for pretty origami paper. Origami is a Japanese art where you fold paper into different shapes, like boats

and birds and hats. Today I was letting Linnie
cut up some paper to make outfits for her
dolls. Because that's what good friends do.

I picked red paper to make a super-sleuth
cape for one of the dolls. That reminded me of
the other clue I had found.

"I also saw a bunch of lists in Mrs. Reese's garage," I told Linnie. "Lists of things like shoes and jackets, maybe for her disguises. But you know what was weird?"

Linnie scrunched her nose as she concentrated on cutting out a princess dress from pink paper. "No, what?"

"One of the lists said *sixteen aprons*," I said. "Why would one person need sixteen things to wear?"

"That *is* strange," Linnie agreed. "Maybe she worked with fifteen other spies?"

"And remember what Sophie said about the musical?" I asked, thinking hard. Something didn't seem right. "The fiddler thing."

"Yeah, I don't know about that," Linnie said.

But we didn't get to talk about it anymore because Mom called us for dinner.

✦ ✦ ✦

The table was set with chopsticks, since that's how we eat Japanese fried noodles. We each had our own chopsticks. Dad's were light brown wood, Mom's were shiny black with a gold moon, Sophie's were blue with orange flowers, and mine were purple with pink hearts. Even Linnie had her own because she ate over a lot. Linnie's were green with pink hearts.

"Ita-daki-masu," Dad said.

"Ita-daki-masu," Linnie said along with me and my family. I smiled a big smile as I dug into my yakisoba. I couldn't wait till tomorrow when we celebrated Girl's Day. Almost everything was perfect. I only wished Sophie were celebrating with us, too.

HAPPY
GIRL'S DAY

The next morning, when I opened my eyes, I was not in my bed. At first I was confused, but then I remembered two important things. Number one, today was Girl's Day. And number two, my best friend, Linnie, had slept over! I was in my purple sleeping bag on the floor of my bedroom. Linnie was sleeping next to me in her green sleeping bag. Except she wasn't in her sleeping bag. I sat up.

I heard whispering coming from the hallway. I crept to the door and listened.

It was Sophie's explaining voice. "So after my mom takes pictures of you and Jasmine in front of the dolls, you get to have a special snack."

Linnie answered in a whisper, "Yes, I know. Jasmine told me about the special mochi."

"Mmmm," Sophie said. "They're shaped like diamonds and layered in pink and white and green. Chewy goodness!"

I jumped into the hallway. "Happy Girl's Day!"

"Happy Girl's Day!" Linnie said. "I didn't want to wake you up, so I was reading in the hall."

Sophie disappeared back into her room.

"Is Sophie celebrating with us?" Linnie watched Sophie's door shut.

I shook my head. "She said she doesn't want to."

"Why not?" Linnie asked as she followed me back into my room. "Girl's Day sounds like fun! Being a girl is awesome!"

"Right?" I said. "It doesn't make any sense."

I thought about how Sophie kept talking about Girl's Day, first with me and now with Linnie. I thought about how I had missed clues when Linnie was afraid of the garage. Maybe Sophie still wanted to be part of Girl's Day, even though she wouldn't admit it. I glanced at Linnie. Sometimes people didn't say how they really felt.

Linnie rolled up her sleeping bag while I shoved mine into my closet. That's when I noticed the two kimonos hung side by side. Mom must have put them in there while we were sleeping.

I grinned as I asked Linnie, "Do you want to play dress up this morning?"

She stood up and lifted her chin like she was about to climb a big mountain. "Yes, I will go back to the garage with you."

"You are so brave," I said, "but I meant we can play dress up right here!"

I brought out a kimono. The silky sleeves waved gently as I moved it toward Linnie, as if the kimono was greeting her. "This is for you to wear today."

Linnie's face brightened immediately. "Really?"

"Really!"

Linnie reached for the kimono, but I pulled back, remembering one last step. "Mom needs to help us," I said.

Linnie frowned like she thought we were old enough to get dressed ourselves.

"I know," I said, "but even grownups need help putting on kimonos. They have a lot of layers and there is a proper way to put them on."

Linnie smiled again. "Okay."

Mom helped us get dressed. First, we put on the white under-kimono. Then Mom helped us put on the pretty printed kimono. The white collar of the under-kimono had to poke up around the edge. The kimono had to wrap left over right. (There are a lot of rules to wearing a kimono!) Next we put on the obi, or belt, and Mom tied it all fancy in the back.

Once we were fully dressed, Linnie and I stood next to each other and looked in the mirror. We were almost the same height. She had brown hair and I had black. We each had the same goofy smile on our face. Her kimono was red with a white fan and cranes. Mine was white with purple flowers. We held hands and squeezed.

In the living room, Mom took pictures of me and Linnie next to the dolls. While I smiled for Mom's camera, Sophie poked around the corner. But when she saw me looking at her, she ducked away.

Mom went to the kitchen to get our snack ready. Linnie and I

STEP 1

STEP 2

STEP 3

stayed with the dolls. Tomorrow, Mom would pack them up and I'd have to wait another year to see them again. Next year felt like a very long time away. If I were Sophie and didn't get to do Girl's Day, I would be sad.

I knew that no matter how nicely I asked, Sophie would say she didn't want to join in. She thought dolls were for babies and she thought she was too grown-up for Girl's Day. She liked to be a know-it-all. If only I could be as bossy as she is and make her celebrate with us.

That gave me an idea.

"I'll be right back," I said to Linnie.

Sophie stood in the hall outside the kitchen, watching Mom.

"Hey," I said.

Sophie spun around. "What do you want?"

"Can you help me explain to Linnie which dolls are which?" I said, even though I knew.

"Boy, you sure have a bad memory," Sophie said.

My big sister followed me back to the living room and pointed to each doll, naming them like I had done for Linnie two days ago. Fortunately, Linnie didn't say a peep to Sophie.

"This one is my favorite," Linnie said, pointing to a court lady holding a tray.

"I like this one," I said, pointing to a musician with a little drum. My finger hovered over the drum. If I moved a little closer I could tap it, but Mom would not be happy about that. Maybe someday I could help her with the dolls.

"I like the empress the best," Sophie said. "She's the most powerful."

Sophie pushed her way between me and Linnie. She sat down and straightened the miniature bowls.

"Come get your treats," Mom called.

When the three of us walked into the kitchen, Mom smiled. "How nice to have all my girls with me here today!"

On two plates were the diamond-shaped  mochi in layers of pink and white and green. Mom put a third mochi on another plate just for Sophie.

Sophie had said she didn't want to celebrate Girl's Day, but I think she just wanted to show she was a big girl. Kind of like how I wanted to prove I wasn't a baby by making mochi with my family on New Year's. Maybe I was a good detective after all. I just had to pay close attention to the clues.

That reminded me of what Mrs. Reese had said about wishing *she* could celebrate Girl's Day.

"What are we doing for our special day?" I asked Mom.

"We're going on a picnic at the park," Mom said.

"Can we invite Mrs. Reese?" I asked.

"That is an excellent idea," Mom said.

SUPER SLEUTH

The mochi was sweet and delicious. I wished we could eat a hundred more, but Mom was on a schedule. She told me, Linnie, and Sophie to sit down in front of the doll display (again). Sophie complained, but not *too* hard. Mom took a bunch more pictures, and Sophie smiled.

After Linnie and I changed back into our regular clothes, we stopped by Sophie's room before going to Mrs. Reese's to invite her to our picnic.

"What do you two want?" Sophie asked, but in her nice voice.

"What was it you said about the fiddler on the roof?" I asked.

"Oh, that it's the name of a musical," Sophie said. "We're studying theater in class. A musical is like a play but acted out with songs in front of a live audience."

I thought about the papers I'd found in the garage that looked like little movie posters.

"Is *Annie Get Your Gun* a musical? What about *Oklahoma!*?" I asked.

"I don't know about the first one, but the second one is a musical for sure."

"What are some other plays?" I asked.

Sophie tapped her finger on her chin. "*Our Town. Romeo and Juliet.*"

I glanced at Linnie. "Do you want to stop by the garage first before visiting Mrs. Reese?"

"You're being a super sleuth, aren't you?" Linnie said with a smile.

✦ ✦ ✦

We ran over to Mrs. Reese's together.

I swung open the garage door and turned on the light. Linnie stepped in behind me. Close behind me. I led her to the box that held the folders. I opened the box and found the little posters. Linnie and I flipped through them.

"There's *Our Town*," Linnie exclaimed, pointing to a green flyer.

"And here's *Romeo and Juliet*," I said. "And look! *Alice in Wonderland*. I know that story."

"What does this mean?" Linnie asked.

I thought about the lists of clothes I had found. "What if all these clothes weren't disguises, but costumes?" I said. "Like the ones we made for your paper dolls?"

"Oh!" Linnie said.

"Maybe Mrs. Reese made costumes for people!"

"You're so smart, Jasmine!" Linnie said.

"I couldn't have done it without you," I said.

"Really?"

"Yes! I only thought about costumes because you wanted to make outfits for your dolls!" I said. "We are a good team!"

"I like that," Linnie said.

"But let's find out for sure," I said.

We put everything away neatly and went to

Mrs. Reese's door. *Wowee zowee!* Something smelled really chocolaty and yummy.

"We would like to invite you to come on our Girl's Day picnic," I said when Mrs. Reese answered the door. The chocolate smell was even stronger. She was wearing a white apron. I wondered if it was from her box in the garage.

"Thank you! That would be lovely," she said  with a smile. "I just baked some brownies, without nuts, the way you like them. I can bring them to your picnic."

"Can we ask you a question?" I asked.

"Of course," Mrs. Reese said.

"Are those clothes in your garage costumes for plays?" I asked.

Mrs. Reese's eyes went wide and she smiled big. "Did you figure that out yourself?"

"I had help," I said, nudging Linnie, who giggled. "We saw the posters in one of the boxes, and the lists of clothes. And Sophie is studying plays in her class. And Linnie likes to make costumes for her dolls."

"I'm impressed," Mrs. Reese said. "You took all those clues and figured it out. Yes, I used to be a costume designer for a theater."

"You really are a super sleuth," Linnie said to me.

"And you're a super–best friend," I replied.

✶ ✶ ✶

A few minutes later, while Sophie and Linnie looked at the Girl's Day dolls one last time, I went to the kitchen to tell Mom that Mrs. Reese would be joining us.

Mom handed me the cloth napkins while she packed sandwiches into the picnic basket.

"I'm glad you and Linnie made up," Mom said. "And I'm glad Sophie decided to celebrate with us. Did you have something to do with that?"

"Maybe," I said as I folded the napkins. "I think she wanted to be with us, but wanted to act too grown-up for Girl's Day at the same time. I wish things didn't have to change."

"I know what you mean." Mom took the folded napkins and put them in the basket. "I love celebrating with you girls, but I know it can't stay the same forever. You're both growing up. When I was a little girl, I didn't ever want Girl's Day to be different, but now I get to celebrate with my daughters. That makes me very happy."

"Are you sad you don't get to celebrate with Obaachan anymore since she lives in Japan?" I asked.

"I miss her," Mom said, "but change doesn't have to be a bad thing. Growing up, like you wanting to make mochi, is a part of life. Just make sure you're doing things because you want to, not because of what others might think."

I nodded. Sophie might still like dolls, but she was worried that playing with them might make her look like a baby. If she wasn't so worried about what other people thought, she could just have fun.

"I like our tradition of Girl's Day," I said. "I like hanging out with you and with Sophie, because we don't get to do that a lot. But I also like hanging out with Linnie. Even if that's not tradition."

"Me, too," Mom said. "But the nice thing

about change and growing up is getting to make *new* traditions." She smiled, holding out her hand. I grabbed it, and we walked together to get Sophie and Linnie for our picnic. I hopped with excitement half the way.

My big weekend plans had turned out perfectly: I had solved the mystery of Mrs. Reese's past. Sophie had joined in on our celebration.

Mrs. Reese was coming to our picnic and was bringing brownies! Mom was happy. And best of all, Linnie and I were still the very best of friends.

It didn't take a super sleuth to see that this really was the best Girl's Day ever! I couldn't wait to see what next year's would be like. It might be different, but it would still be super-great!

AUTHOR'S NOTE

Girl's Day, also called Hina-Matsuri (*hee-nah-mah-tsoo-ree*), or Doll Festival, takes place on March 3. It is a special day in Japan to celebrate girls. Girls dress up in their best kimonos (*kee-moh-noh*). Families display a special set of dolls. These dolls represent the imperial court. At the very top step of the platform are the emperor and empress. On the lower steps are the court ladies, guards and ministers, musicians, and miniature furniture. Families also display peach blossoms in the home for beauty. There are special diamond-shaped mochi (*moh-chee*; Japanese treats made out of sweet rice) colored in pink, white, and green layers. Pink symbolizes the flowers of spring, white stands for purity, and green is for new growth. It is thought that this holiday originated from a tradition of floating paper dolls in a river to get rid of bad luck.

Kimonos are beautiful robe-like silk garments worn in Japan. In the past, people wore kimonos every day. Today, people usually wear kimonos only during special festivals or when they get married. There are many layers to a traditional kimono. First comes the juban (*ju-bahn*), or under-kimono. Tabi (*tah-bee*) are socks that are like mittens for your toes so you can wear the special shoes called geta (*gheh-tah*). The kimono comes next and overlaps left over right. The last step is to put on the obi (*oh-bee*), or sash belt, with a fancy bow tied in back. The kimono is wrapped tightly. Both men and women wear kimonos, but women's are brightly colored and are decorated with beautiful designs while, typically, men's kimonos are plainer.

There is also a special day for boys, called Boy's Day, or Tango no Sekku (*Tahn-goh noh Sehk-koo*), which is celebrated on May 5. In 1948, the Japanese government announced that May 5 would be a national holiday to celebrate all children. Now it is called Children's Day, or Kodomo no Hi (*Koh-doh-moh noh hee*).

ORIGAMI PAPER DOLL

SUPER-FUN TO MAKE WITH YOUR BEST FRIENDS!

MATERIALS

- Origami paper or any square piece of paper
- Markers
- Colored pencils or crayons

INSTRUCTIONS

1. Lay the paper flat. If you're using printed origami paper, put the plain side facing up.

2. Fold the bottom 1/3 of the way up.

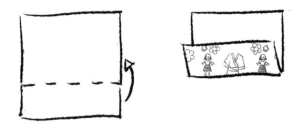

3. Turn the paper so the folded part is on the left.

4. Fold the bottom 1/3 of the way up.

5. Turn the paper so the plain/blank end is pointed up.

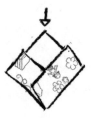

6. Flip the paper over.

7. Fold the bottom point up to make a small triangle.

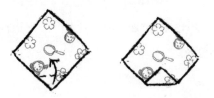

8. Flip the paper over again.

9. The plain section is the doll's face. Draw your doll's face. You can also decorate the rest of your doll.

10. When you're done, you can stand your doll up using the small bent triangle at the back.

Turn the page for a sneak peek of . . .

JASMINE TOGUCHI

MOCHI QUEEN

DEBBI MICHIKO FLORENCE   PICTURES BY ELIZABET VUKOVIĆ

BE SURE TO LOOK FOR

JASMINE TOGUCHI
DRUMMER
GIRL
COMING SOON!

A TERRIFIC IDEA

It was safest for me to hide in my room. Mom was scrubbing the guest bathroom. Dad was getting the cardboard boxes from the garage. My big sister, Sophie, was sweeping the kitchen floor. I waited for my chance to escape the cleaning frenzy.

I, Jasmine Toguchi, do *not* like to clean! But I do like to climb trees, eat dessert, and make messes. I'd rather do any of those things right now.

I peeked out my bedroom window. Dad has moved into the backyard! I tiptoed out of my room. Nobody in the hall! I ran to the front door. But just as I put my hand on the doorknob, I heard footsteps behind me.

"Jasmine Toguchi, where do you think you're going?"

I turned slowly to face my mother.

"We need to clean the house before everyone arrives tomorrow," Mom said. "Now go help your sister."

Walnuts! This was *exactly* what I was trying to avoid. Helping Sophie would mean that I did all the work while she bossed me around.

"I already finished sweeping," Sophie announced from the next room. Scattered across the kitchen floor, small mounds of dust and bits of trash sat like sand dunes on the beach. Except this was no vacation. "You can pick it all up. I'll let you know if you do a good job."

Sophie is two years older than me. She thinks that makes her my boss. If that weren't annoying enough, she also gets to do everything before me. She started school first. She learned to read first. She even started piano lessons last year, and I have to wait another year. Not that I really want to play the piano.

Sophie was always the expert. She thought she was smarter and better than me. Just once, I wished I could do something first. Just once, I wanted to be the expert.

As I swept the piles into the dustpan, Sophie climbed up onto the kitchen stool. It was like being higher up made her more in charge. This meant barking commands at me while she picked at the chipped polish on her fingernails.

"You missed a pile!"

"Stop sweeping so hard! You're making dust fly into the air!"

"Don't spill or you'll have to clean it up."

I sighed and swept.

We were getting ready for mochi-tsuki. Every year, our relatives come over to our house to celebrate New Year's. We spend the entire day making mochi, Japanese sweet rice cakes. It's hard work to make mochi, but there's a reward—eating the gooey treat afterward.

Actually, all the other relatives do the hard work. In my family, you had to be at least ten years old to make mochi. This year would be Sophie's first time getting to help. I'm only eight. Once again, Sophie would do something before I did. By the time I was ten and got to make mochi, too, she would be the expert and boss me around. That would take all the fun out of it.

This year, just like last year, I would be stuck babysitting.

I bent over, scooped, and walked to the trash can to empty the dustpan. I did this a hundred times, at least.

I wished I could help with mochi-tsuki. I didn't want

to watch DVDs with my four-year-old cousins. It wasn't fair. I was big enough to make mochi.

"I'm going to help make mochi," I said to Sophie.

She kept picking at her orange nails. "You're too little. You'll only get in the way."

"I'm big enough." Yesterday I noticed I came up to Sophie's chin. During the summer I came up to her shoulder. I was growing!

"Just wait your turn," she said.

This year, Sophie would sit at the table in the backyard with Mom and all the other women. She would probably get to sit right next to Obaachan, our grandma who came from Japan every year for the holidays.

"Stop pouting and finish cleaning," Sophie said. "You'll get your turn at mochi-tsuki when you're ten."

I wished there was something I could do before her. Something she could never do.

I swept up another dust pile. Suddenly, I got

an idea. It was tradition for Dad, the uncles, and the boy cousins to turn the cooked rice into the sticky mochi by pounding it in a stone bowl with a big wooden hammer. That's what I could do. I could pound mochi with the boys!

"What are you grinning about?" Sophie scooted off the stool and took the dustpan from me. "Sweep the floor again to make sure there's nothing left."

You needed to be strong to pound mochi. I was strong. So I swept the floor using all my muscles.

"Stop!" Sophie screeched. "You almost hit me! Mom! Jasmine tried to whack me in the head with the broom!"

Hitting Sophie sounded like good practice for pounding mochi, but I knew it would only get me in trouble.

Just then Mom walked into the kitchen, her forehead wrinkled like it always was when she got annoyed.

"Jasmine Toguchi! You know better than that. Go clean your room if you can't work well with your sister."

I handed the broom to Sophie with a smile and skipped to my room to work on my terrific idea!